For Marc, Calixte, and Radost, my loyal companions on the road …
S. C.

Text and illustration copyright © 2016 Casterman
Translated by Vanessa Miéville

First published in the English language in 2017 by
words & pictures, Part of The Quarto Group
6 Orchard, Lake Forest, CA 92630

A CIP record for the book is available from the Library of Congress.

ISBN: 978-1-91027-748-5

1 3 5 7 9 8 6 4 2

Printed in China

Zidrou • Sébastien Chebret

Bobby's
got a brand-new car

words & **pictures**

It's decided!
Today, Bobby is going to buy himself a car.
A large, beautiful car—one that goes **Vroom!** for real.

The car dealer hurries over.
"Hello!" says Bobby, politely. "I would like to buy a car.
A large, beautiful car—one that goes **Vroom!** for real."

The car dealer shows
him various models.
But Bobby doesn't
really like any of them.

Suddenly, he spots his
dream car: a convertible.

"Good idea!" says the car dealer approvingly.
"It would be a shame not to enjoy this beautiful sunshine."

Bobby pays with his magic card
(the one that pays for everything).

"Thank you, Sir!" says the car dealer, delighted. "Goodbye, Sir! Until next time!"

Bobby drives his new car.
The car goes **Vroom!**
It goes **Beep-beep!** and **Eeeeeee!**
All the noises that cars make when they are happy.

Bobby puts on some
very loud music.
The policeman waves.
The traffic lights turn green.
Even the train stops to watch
him drive past.

Bobby fills the car with gas.
He pays with his magic card
(the one that pays for everything).

Bobby collects his mom from school
where she works as a teacher.
Mom sits in the front, next to Bobby.
"What a beautiful car!" Mom declares.
"I really love the color."
The other teachers seem a bit jealous.

On the way back, Bobby goes to
pick up Dad from work.
Dad has to sit in the back.
"Put your seat belt on!" Bobby tells him.
And he takes off like a rocket.

Bobby drives fast.
Dad feels a bit unwell in the back.
Mom asks Bobby to slow down.

Back home already!
Bobby parks his car inside the garage.
"My car definitely deserves a rest."

Night comes and turns off the lights in the sky.
Tucked up in bed, Bobby thinks about all the
wonderful things he has dreamed up that day.
Then he dreams of what he might do tomorrow.
What if he bought a plane? A large, beautiful plane—
one that goes Whooosh! for real.